TOLLINS
EXPLOSIVE TALES FOR CHILDREN

Conn Iggulden

First published in Great Britain in 2009
by HarperCollins Children's Books
This Large Print edition published by
AudioGO Ltd 2010
by arrangement with
HarperCollins Publishers Ltd

ISBN 978 1405 664219

British Library Cataloguing in Publication Data available

Printed and bound in Great Britain by
CPI Antony Rowe, Chippenham and Eastbourne

For Cameron and Mia
Conn Iggulden

For Maxwell and Darcy
Lizzy Duncan

CONTENTS

BOOK ONE

HOW TO BLOW UP TOLLINS

Chapter One

THE YEAR 1922, DURING THE REIGN OF KING GEORGE V

Tollins are *not* fairies. Though they both have wings, fairies are delicate creatures and much smaller. When he was young, Sparkler accidentally broke one and had to shove it behind a bush before its friends noticed.

In addition, fairies cannot sing B-sharp. They can manage a very nice B-flat, in quite a sweet voice, but B-sharp comes out like a frog being run over by a bicycle. Tollins regard fairies as fluttery show-offs and occasionally use them to wipe out the insides of cups. Tollins are also a lot less fragile than fairies. In fact, the word 'fragile' can't really be used about them at all. They are about as fragile as a housebrick.

Before that summer when the world changed, Sparkler had looked forward to a full life containing nothing more dangerous than wrestling angry bees off flowers, or occasionally dancing with other Tollins at the full moon. He loved to dance, even when he trod on the toes of the others, or tripped over a fairy ring. Fairies never tripped, or fell over, so when they tried to take part, Tollins always began a singing competition instead. In the key of B. If the fairies stamped their little feet and rose to the challenge, they sounded like silver bells being dunked in soup before they gave up. Tollins enjoyed that.

When Sparkler was born, his parents enjoyed a simple life of fluttering around at the bottom of people's gardens. The most exciting thing that had ever happened to them was being chased by two little girls, until they were fortunately distracted by a pony. Adults were no danger. They just *couldn't* see Tollins, even if they were really close.

At first, the Tollins had thought nothing of the serious men with large beards and even larger boots who suddenly seemed to be everywhere, measuring things with bits of string and nodding to each other. Yet in just a short time, they had transformed the little village of Chorleywood. First they had run rails for clanking trains, then they built their firework factory. It had very thick walls and an extremely thin roof, just in case.

The Tollins hadn't minded the fireworks being tested. Some nights, Sparkler had gathered with his parents and grandparents to watch the serious, bearded men light them, one after the other. None of the fireworks went *whee* or had colours back then. [*Some people have suggested that Chinese Tollins were used in fireworks more than a thousand years ago. This is NOT that story.*] They just went *bang* and made the men jump and clap their hands together, almost like the children they had once been.

The 'Great Firework Discovery' had been an accident, really. One of the youngest Tollins had crept too close to a firework on the bench of the factory. While no one was around, the little one climbed into the tube of something called a 'Roman Candle'. Just as he was tasting a pinch of the black powder inside, it all went dark and he was trapped.

The other Tollins searched for him, of course, but there was no sign. That night, the first fireworks were the usual sort, jumping and spluttering, but then the Roman Candle was lit, and the world changed forever.

Sparkler had been there, sitting on a wall with his family. He still remembered the way the Roman Candle leapt into the air, trailing a shower of blue sparks before exploding with a *bang* that knocked one of the men down. The man's beard was on fire when he stood up, but that didn't stop him cheering as he patted the flames out.

In the silence, in the night air, the Tollins heard the voice of the little one they had lost.

'Heeeeelp!' he yelled. The older Tollins looked at each other and their wings vibrated so fast you could hardly see them. They leapt up into the darkness and one of them caught the little Tollin as he fell.

He was bruised but alive, though his

wings were in tatters. Those would grow back in time, but he also seemed to have gone deaf and couldn't understand the questions they were all asking.

'What?' he kept saying. 'I was in the firework! No, *in* it! Didn't you see? What?'

Deep under Chorleywood station, the High Tollin had called a council of seniors together to discuss the problem. While his parents spoke at the meeting, Sparkler had tended to the burned one who kept shouting 'What?' The little one's name had been Cherry, but he insisted they call him 'Roman' after that.

Tollins had come into contact with humans before. They were too curious for their own good and humans always seemed to be doing something *interesting*. Small Tillets were still told the tale of the Tollin who wrestled an apple off a tree and dropped it on the head of a young man sleeping below. The young man's name was Isaac Newton and, as a result, he discovered gravity.

As a young Tillet, Sparkler had even spent time at a school, when he overslept in a satchel. He still cherished the memories of the little book he had brought home, full of big letters and pictures of apples and bees. The bees smiled from the page, which was surprising. In Sparkler's experience, bees had no sense of humour.

Just taking that book had been an enormous risk. After all, the first Tollin law was that *no one* spoke to humans. It always led to trouble, or sometimes gravity. It was better for Tollins if humans didn't know they existed. After all, Tollins weren't fast, or even particularly nimble. Over the years, they had been caught by propellers, run over by lawn mowers and one had become tangled in a kite string until he bit through it. They might not have been fast, but they *were* tough. One of them had even been swallowed by a cat and she survived too, but the less said about that the better.

In the end, the High Tollin decided no lasting harm had been done. He couldn't have known then that the men with beards were more excited about the new kind of firework than they were about big ships, good boots and proper penknives *put together*. Seeing young Roman whoosh above their heads had been the most interesting moment of their lives and they would not rest until they had managed to do it again. If the Tollins had known then about Catherine wheels, perhaps they might have flown to a different part of the country, joining the Dark Tollins of Dorset, or the Mountain Tollins of Wales. They could even have stowed away on a ferry to another country, where Tollins spoke in a strange accent and wore berets. If they had, it would have saved them from headaches, exhaustion, fallen arches and worst of all, *slavery*.

Chapter Two

SERIOUS AND DETERMINED MEN WITH BEARDS

It took almost two years for the bearded men to discover the secret of good fireworks. The Tollins sometimes watched through the windows of the factory as the men rolled the tubes and tried to recreate the magic moment when young Roman had almost blown himself to pieces.

Sparkler had snorted with laughter as the men tried adding pieces of their beards, scraps of their jackets and even tiny snips from their boots, though that batch of fireworks just smelled awful. If he had thought about it, he might have realised that no matter how many times the firework men failed, they just shrugged their shoulders and *tried again*. You only have to wrestle a bee off a flower once or twice before he goes away, but the bearded men were serious *and* determined.

The events of that summer started with two boys from a local house. They had spotted Sparkler's parents sunbathing on a daffodil and instead of standing in amazement as children usually do, or even running back to the house for a shoebox and butterfly net, they yelled and whistled and raised such a commotion that Sparkler's father fell into a rose bush.

The boys' parents didn't believe the story at first, but their father had worked in the fireworks factory for a long time. He scratched his beard and tapped his boots on the ground, looking very thoughtful. He looked at the garden and he looked at the firework factory which was just next door. He considered lighting his pipe, which he couldn't do in the factory in case he blew the roof off.

'Well, I've tried everything else,' he said to himself. After all, *something* had made that Roman Candle better than all the others. Some special ingredient had made it soar upwards, like the dreams of bearded men.

He knew his two sons weren't

handsome or clever. They were in fact the sort of boys who collect beetles and try to race them for money, but they didn't tell lies, or at least, not very often. The bearded man didn't think they would make up something as strange as a little winged creature sleeping on a daffodil, or even one who fell in a rose bush and used very bad language indeed.

It wasn't long before the bearded man was creeping about at the bottom of his garden, armed with a net. That didn't work of course. He couldn't see them and the Tollins just flitted about without a care in the world. Some of the young Tillets were trying to make fairy-powered roller skates, but the fairies kept getting squashed. Later, when Sparkler looked back on those innocent days, with the little piles of flat fairies, it made him sad. It had been a happy time.

It was a simple blue glass filter that made the difference. The Tollins kept away from the two boys, but they didn't try to hide from an adult—they had never needed to.

They saw that the bearded man had made himself a pair of glasses and they saw the way he kept changing the lenses and peering into the bushes, but they fluttered on, drinking nectar and laughing at the way Sparkler's dad couldn't sit down. The first they knew of the blue glass filter was when three of them were scooped up in a jam jar and the lid screwed down. They were trapped! The bearded man shouted in excitement and even considered a little dance of his own, before he remembered his wife was watching from the house.

That night, the Tollins gathered along the walls of the testing yard and watched three green rockets whoosh up to the stars before exploding with a noise that sounded a bit like thunder, but a lot more like the end of the world. Their friends had fluttered down with burnt wings, shouting 'What?' just as poor Roman had done.

The next morning, the Tollins were woken by *dozens* of bearded men shouting and stamping around. All of them worked for the factory and all carried jam jars and wore glasses with blue lenses. As the sun rose, Tollins were snatched off petals, flowers and flowerpots. They'd be quietly snoring and suddenly *whoosh*, they were in a net, and *pop*, they were in a jam jar. The fairies didn't seem to mind the sudden loss of their companions. The blue filters didn't reveal *fairies* at all. Some of them sang a farewell song that they called 'Goodbye to the summer (with burping frogs) in B-sharp'.

The bearded men lined up the jam jars on the workbenches of the factory and the poor Tollins looked mournfully at each other. They all knew what was going to happen. They eyed the rows of cardboard tubes uneasily, but there was nothing they could do. One by one, they were plucked out by huge fingers and stuffed into fireworks.

Some of them went legs first. The unluckiest ones went head first.

Sparkler was one of the unlucky ones. He found himself upside down in something called a 'Moon Rocket'. For a while, he comforted himself with the thought that Roman had survived the experience. Surely he too would live through the explosion to come.

One of the men tapped Sparkler's tube and the shivering Tollin heard the words, even through the layers of cardboard.

'That's enough for the demonstration,' said the man. The voice was very low and deep, so it seemed to go on for a long time. To humans, Tollin voices sounded a little bit like the whine of a fly. They tried to swat them when they crept up to an ear. Sparkler concentrated as the voice boomed somewhere close. He could not hear if the owner had a beard, but he imagined one anyway.

'After this,' he heard, 'we'll be the most famous fireworks factory in England!'

His companion had a slightly less bearded voice. 'How are we going to get enough of them though? They'll run out eventually.'

'We'll comb the south of England for them, now we have the blue glasses,' his cheerful friend replied. 'We've found forty in just a few gardens. If we get the job for Buckingham Palace, we'll have buyers queuing down the street. We'll make our fortune!'

Sparkler seethed in his tube. The bearded men didn't realise Tollins could survive being used in fireworks! They honestly thought they were going to blow them up! He was horrified and then, after a bit of thought, he was horrified again. It wouldn't be long before the bearded men found out that Tollins could be used *over and over and over again*.

The future looked dark, though to be fair, almost everything looks dark when you are wedged upside down in a cardboard tube.

CHAPTER THREE

THE VITAL IMPORTANCE OF SALAMI

Sparkler survived his first trip in a Moon Rocket. He had quite a lot of time to think about his situation before his tube was lit. Stunned and deafened, he fell for a long time before landing on the roof of Buckingham Palace in London. The bearded men had impressed the king with their new fireworks and Sparkler had been launched as a result. Three more Tollins landed among the pipes and tiles of the roof and rested there with Sparkler. It took almost two months for their wings to grow back.

By the time they were ready to fly home to Chorleywood, Sparkler had formed one important question that needed an answer. It didn't worry the men in the factory. They were happy enough gathering up Tollins from miles around and if they even noticed some of the them were the same, it didn't seem to trouble them. For Sparkler, though, it was important. *Why* were Tollin fireworks better than the normal kind?

It was while trudging through Somerset on his way home for the third time that he noticed something different about himself.

Tollins have dust on them. It wouldn't be right to call it 'fairy dust', as fairies don't actually have any. It's Tollin dust. Tollins don't think about it much, any more than you think about your eyebrows, or a moth thinks about moth dust, though that exists as well. For Tollins, it's a light powder on their wings and skin that drifts behind them as they fly. Sparkler was the first to notice that *all the dust had gone* after every trip in a firework. Somehow, the bright colours and explosion used it up. It came back, thank goodness, just as their wings grew back, but Sparkler thought it had to be important. He was almost cheerful as he walked through the Somerset village of Taunton in the moonlight.

When he reached Chorleywood at last, he gathered some of the other Tollins at an old oak tree on Chorleywood Common. In the tunnels under the station, he knew the High Tollin would again be in deep discussion with his council, so deep it would be difficult to wake them for dinner. Sparkler knew they'd never listen to him, so he gathered the ones he knew and trusted. Some had been taken for the latest batch of fireworks. His friend Grunion was still in a tube and his parents were somewhere over Margate, if Sparkler had read the factory supply lists correctly. That little book with its pictures of apples and bees had come in handy there. So had the children's dictionary he had borrowed the previous year. It made his brain fizz to look through the pages, like a . . . well, like a firework, with ears.

When the Tollins were all settled, Sparkler took a deep breath.

'It's the dust,' he told them, making himself comfortable on a fairy cushion. It squeaked a bit, but he ignored it.

'Whatever it is, it burns off when they light the tubes. That's what makes the colours and *that's* why Tollin fireworks are so good.'

The other Tollins shuffled and stared at each other, then back at him. They were a bedraggled bunch compared to the happy Tollins he had known before the factory came. In the end, it fell to an old Tollin named Briar to speak for all of them. Briar had refused to call himself by one of the new names. His first experience of the factory had been on a Catherine wheel and 'Catherine' didn't suit him, not even a little bit. Spinning round at high speed had not been enjoyable at *all*. In fact, he hadn't walked in a straight line since that day.

'You could be right, lad. But it doesn't help us, does it?'

Sparkler blinked at the old Tollin.

'Of course it does! If we can find out what the dust is, we can show the bearded men! They wouldn't have to use us if they could get the dust somewhere else, would they?'

The crowd perked up at this news,

but Sparkler went on.

'Even if we can't make it, they could just scrape it off! We'd never have to travel in a rocket again!'

They cheered that idea, but then Briar cleared his throat like a dog enjoying a boiled sweet.

'Have you forgotten the First Law, old son? *We do not speak to humans*. It leads to trouble and, sometimes, gravity.'

Sparkler nodded slowly.

'I haven't forgotten, Briar, but this is an emergency. I'll be the one to break the law. If it means trouble later, it'll fall on my head alone.'

'The High Tollin won't approve, you know,' Briar said thoughtfully.

'That, Briar,' Sparkler replied, 'is why I am not going to tell him.'

Briar sucked his teeth for a bit and Sparkler went on quickly before the old Tollin could think of anything else.

'There are different kinds of humans,' Sparkler told the crowd. 'I've seen ones who drive lorries and ones who build walls.'

He had kept his best thought till last

and his eyes sparkled, which was, incidentally, how he got his name. No one had yet tried strapping a Tollin to a sparkler, thank goodness.

'They have teachers and doctors, vets and dentists, but I've also learned the word for ones who look at things and work them out.'

He stared around at the forty, battered Tollins and for the first time in ages, he saw hope in their eyes.

'Scientists! We need to become Tollin scientists.'

Even old Briar gave up some of his dust when Sparkler came around with a scraper and a cup. Finding a way to set the mixture on fire was harder than anyone had expected, but they managed to carry away a box of matches from someone's kitchen without being spotted. Sparkler set up his own workbench under the hollow oak and the rest of the Tollins waited for results. When he lit the first batch of dust and blew his eyebrows off, they heard his cheer right across Chorleywood. He was pleased it had worked. He was also surprised, but without his eyebrows, no one could tell.

After that, Sparkler had plenty of volunteers to help him. Anyone who wasn't in a jam jar or a firework spent their spare time digging. They brought just about anything to Sparkler, from brown coloured rock, to red coloured rock and even a bit of reddish-brown coloured rock. He tried to light each piece, but nothing worked. After that, they raided the house where they had found the matches, coming away with baking powder, bath salts, salami slices, vinegar and a host of other things.

Each night, the Tollins would donate a scraping of dust to his experiments and if anyone noticed the fireworks no longer had quite the whizz and zip of earlier months, no one said anything. The High Tollin was still discussing the problem with his council under the station. Enormous plates of sandwiches were sent in to help them come up with a solution.

In the depths of winter, Sparkler looked at a pile of grubby crystals. According to the packet of salami, it was something called 'sodium nitrate'.

It had been very hard to get it out of the meat. He'd boiled the salami and cooled it, shredded and dissolved it—and he didn't know if it was any good, even then. Tollin dust was gold and this was grey, but he still leaned away as he lit his match, having learned once how slowly eyebrows grow back.

The whoosh of yellow flame lasted for just an instant and left bright flashes in front of his eyes as he staggered out of the old oak. He had yellow! If he managed blue and red as well, he would have saved them all.

CHAPTER FOUR

TALKING TO BEARDS

It was a tense moment in the firework factory. Just getting the bearded men to notice him and listen had taken a month. Sparkler had been launched over the southern counties three more times before he finally caught their attention in the most drastic way possible. As they'd stuffed him into a firework, he'd lit a match and hung on. Even then, he'd almost blown himself out of the tube in a flare of beautiful blue. That brought them running, as you might expect. Bearded men *love* fireworks, but they don't like them going off on the workbench, not at all.

Sparkler had to slow his voice down to speak to them, until it felt like he was singing the deepest notes he could manage. He had seen a great ear coming close and discovered that bearded men grow a surprising amount of hair in those as well. Yet they listened and somehow, they understood what he was trying to say.

The foreman of the factory was there of course, dressed in a black suit and a waistcoat with a gold chain hanging from it. The factory was being painted and it wasn't even open, but all the bearded men had come to watch Sparkler demonstrate his firework powders. To a man, they all wore blue glasses and squinted at the Tollins gathered on the workbench.

It was a small group of Tollins. Only a few had dared to watch Sparkler break the First Law and actually speak to a human. Most of the others were in the tunnels under the station, with lots of witnesses to show they had never been anywhere near the firework factory.

Roman and Briar had refused to stay away. They moved the paint tins back to give Sparkler room as he dragged the matchbox forward.

Nervously, Sparkler said 'Sodium Nitrate' as slowly and deeply as he could. It was a word from a human book and the men nodded and raised their eyebrows at each other. After that, Sparkler said 'Copper Chloride' and finally, 'Strontium Carbonate', which took *ages* to say at that speed. As he finished each one, he touched a lit match to a pile and was rewarded by a series of *oohs* and *aahs* from the bearded men. One of them said *whee* as well, but he was *shushed* by the rest. The shadowy factory was lit in yellow, blue and a lovely red before Sparkler finally slumped back onto the matchbox and waited. He had worked through the night to prepare the display and he was exhausted.

The foreman strode over to him and peered down through thick, blue glasses.

'All right, lad,' he said. 'Show me how you did it and we'll do it your way.'

The Tollins cheered. One of them danced on the workbench. Roman even climbed onto one of the paint tins and danced on that. As Sparkler raised his hands in triumph, he saw the lid spin round and Roman disappeared into the pot. Those who saw cried out in fear. Some of them turned to the bearded men, thinking this was perhaps a new trap, but those days were over.

The foreman himself lifted Roman out of the paint pot and put him on the bench where he stood in a puddle of the stuff. The Tollins began cheering again, but Sparkler saw a look of astonishment cross the foreman's face.

The painted walls of the fireworks factory were white. The paint in the tins was white. The only bit that wasn't white was the puddle around Roman. That was the most marvellous shade of purple anyone had ever seen.

'Look at the colour of that paint!' said one of the bearded men, excitedly.

'Oh no,' said Sparkler. 'Not again.'

BOOK TWO

SPARKLER AND THE PURPLE DEATH

CHAPTER ONE

HOW AMPUTATION CAN BE A BLESSING

Sparkler stamped his feet to get rid of the snow. His wings had frozen again. As he blew his nose on a fairy handkerchief, he was cold and miserable. You would probably prefer to believe that a fairy handkerchief was a piece of silky cloth *made* by the fairies. That is definitely one possibility. The fairies had even offered to make such an item from spider web, but Sparkler preferred the old-fashioned kind. He stuffed the snotty fairy back in his coat pocket and knocked on the door of Grunion's tiny house, in a hill by Darvell's Pond.

The wind howled around him as he waited. It was still autumn, but Chorleywood Common was covered in whiteness. The owls and foxes were out as the sun set and Sparkler looked around nervously as the door opened and young Grunion beckoned him inside.

Sparkler waited while Grunion bolted the little door, then he followed the healer down a long passage into the hill, the tap-thump of Grunion's false foot echoing behind him. The air grew warmer with every step and with relief, Sparkler felt his wings begin to thaw. It was not long before he was seated in Grunion's workshop, looking in fascination at all the odd things in jars. Some of them looked back. The fire crackled and he draped his fairy handkerchief over the mantlepiece to dry out. He heard it sneeze in the silence.

'Is it finished then?' Grunion asked. His father had been famous as a healer, though mostly it was famous in the sense that *everyone* knew it was a bad idea to go to him if you were sick. Grunion senior had died at the end of summer, taken by an owl.

'I have finished the copying,' Sparkler replied, patting a bag at his waist. 'I have here the very first book of proper medicine ever created.'

'*Human* medicine,' Grunion said reluctantly, holding out his hand for it.

'They know more than we do,' Sparkler replied with a shrug, pulling out the book. He handed it to Grunion and held his breath as the Tollin flicked through the pages.

'Did you do the drawings as well?' Grunion asked. He held out a picture of a very odd-looking daffodil. Sparkler blushed.

'I did my best. It can't *all* apply to Tollins, but some of these plants could be used to reduce fevers and dull pain. It has to be better than amputation.'

It was a sensitive subject. Grunion's father had cured his son's athlete's foot by removing the foot. Grunion senior had also recommended it as a cure for ingrown toenails, tennis elbow and dandruff.

'Amputation works, though,' Grunion said warily. He lifted his false foot as he spoke, so that Sparkler could see the finely carved little toes. 'Saves in shoes, too.'

'I'm sure your father was . . . a great Tollin, but there is more to medicine than just removing the bit that hurts. This book says so, anyway.'

'I'll look at it, but I'm not promising anything. My father always said that sudden death teaches people a very valuable lesson.'

Sparkler said nothing. He still remembered the fancy dress party at the end of summer. Grunion senior had gone as a mouse. Presumably the owl had worked out its mistake eventually, but it was too late by then. Come to think of it, there probably *was* a lesson in there somewhere.

In the distance, a dull thumping broke the peaceful silence.

'Expecting someone?' Sparkler asked.

Grunion looked up from the book of herbs and shook his head.

Both Tollins walked back to the door in the tiny hill. Made of snail-shell, it was slightly translucent, but Grunion could only see two dark shapes standing outside.

He pulled back the bolt and let in a breath of frozen air. Two large Tollins stood there, stamping their feet.

Sparkler blinked as they grinned at him, showing too many teeth. They carried spears and wore blue tunics only slightly stained with gravy.

'Thought we'd find you here,' said the first.

'May I help you?' Sparkler said, bewildered.

'Ho yes, you *may* help us,' said the second one. He was larger and if anything, slightly more menacing. The first one snickered, which was not a pleasant sound. He did not in fact, look like a pleasant Tollin.

'You may help us by accompanying us back to the High Tollin so he can shout at you and throw you in a cell.'

'I'm sorry?' said Sparkler in amazement.

'You can apologise later, my lad. Right now, you are coming with us.'

'No, I meant it as an expression of surprise, like "Well I never",' Sparkler said. 'Are you sure you have the right Tollin?'

'You *are* the Tollin who spoke to humans? Who *conversed* with them?'

'Yes, but I don't think . . .'

Whatever Sparkler had been going to say was lost as the two guards leapt at him, dragging a rough sack over his shoulders. In just moments, he was tied like a parcel.

'Is it necessary to be so rough?' Grunion said in horror.

The two guards looked at each other.

'Well no,' the large one replied, 'but it's part of the job, you see. Even the manual is called 'A Rough Guide to Guarding' so it's sort of rule number one.'

'Will there be a trial, then?' Grunion asked. It had happened so quickly, he was still trying to catch up.

'Ho yes, a trial, very important. We tell everyone what he did and then the High Tollin decides to execute him. It's all very proper and legal, don't you worry about *that*.'

'*Do* something, Grunion!' said the parcel. The guards cracked their knuckles in anticipation and Grunion decided that standing with his mouth open was as much as he was prepared to try at that time.

As Sparkler was dragged away, Grunion found his courage and called after him.

'You must keep your hopes alive, my friend. Though they throw you in the deepest dungeon with only beetles for company, there will surely . . .'

He realised Sparkler was too far away to hear through a sack.

'Blast,' said Grunion, and shut the door to think.

Chapter Two

THE HIGH TOLLIN MAKES THINGS QUITE CLEAR

Deep under Chorleywood station, the Hall of the High Tollin was warm and busy. Sparkler was jostled through the tunnels before finally being thrown down onto a cold floor. The sack was whipped off him and he blinked at the sudden light. It was not a large hall, as halls go. Moles would have found it a bit low-ceilinged for a centre of government. Most Tollins only ever went there to be named, married and marked dead, or at least 'absent, probably foxed or owled'. Winter was hard on Tollins.

Sparkler rose slowly to his feet.

'I think there has been some sort of misunderstanding . . .' he began.

'*Silence* in the presence of the High Tollin!' one of the guards roared in his ear. Page two of the manual: 'The Importance of Volume', presumably.

Sparkler had read it. He read everything. He vaguely recalled some worrying sections on 'Community Guarding—the Importance of a Good Kicking'.

Sparkler remained silent, staring up at the little crowd of Tollins on the raised area at the end of the hall. They surrounded the oldest Tollin he had ever seen. When Sparkler had been named, old Gristle had been in the chair, so this was a new High Tollin. He had a face like a walnut with a beard and enormous eyebrows. From somewhere in the bushy hair, the High Tollin glared out at him.

'So this is the one who broke our laws, is it?' he demanded. As Sparkler watched, the wrinkled old Tollin grew purple with rage. He looked as if he wanted to rise from his seat, but one of his feet was swollen and wrapped in bandages. Grunion senior would have had it right off, Sparkler thought. He stared at the foot with great interest.

'Answer the High Tollin!' the guard roared again. Page 6: 'Communicating with the Public'.

'I did speak to the owner of the firework factory, yes,' Sparkler began.

'Condemned from his own marf, sah!' the second guard snapped, saluting. 'Shall I execute him now?'

'Marf?' the High Tollin said.

'Clear as day, sah!' the guard went on proudly. The High Tollin summoned his advisors and muttered for a few moments.

'Right, I see. Well why didn't he just *say* that?' he whispered. Sparkler watched in horror as the High Tollin cleared his throat. 'Then in view of the confession, it is only for me to pronounce sentence. Then lunch.'

'I *had* to talk to them!' Sparkler blurted out. 'We were being used in fireworks! As slaves! What choice did I have?' To his surprise, there was a murmur of agreement from the galleries and he looked up to see many Tollins watching the scene.

'As *sla-aves*!' Sparkler said louder, for those at the back.

The High Tollin frowned at this attempt to appeal to the crowd. When he spoke again, his voice was low and poisonous.

'Tollins have rules, you know,' he said. 'Some things are obviously forbidden to us, like murder or Wednesdays. We are not creatures of chaos, after all. Yet above all that is the First Law. We *do not speak to humans*. The law is not to be bent, young Tollin. It does not matter if you 'really needed' to speak to one, or that you 'just had to have a quick word'. The law is clear, the law is *truth*.'

'But you can't possibly . . .' Sparkler interrupted.

'Take him to the cells,' the High Tollin said. 'You will . . . *nyaaargh!*'

Everyone froze at the sudden yell of agony from the High Tollin.

'Sah?' the guard said, uncertainly. Sparkler stared as the High Tollin turned to his closest advisor.

'Would you mind awfully removing your hand from my leg? You seem to be resting on it.' The advisor jumped clear as if he had touched a hot stove.

'Thank you *so* much,' the High Tollin murmured with icy politeness. 'It's the gout, you see, otherwise I wouldn't have dreamed of mentioning it.'

The ancient Tollin gathered his thoughts once more.

'Humans are dangerous!' he snapped. 'We survive only because they do not know we exist. Then what happens, after centuries of peace? They wear blue glasses and find us in every garden! The humiliation of it! We could have hidden ourselves in the winter tunnels, but what did you do? You spoke to them! You showed them how to make better fireworks!'

'We can learn many things from humans,' Sparkler tried.

'Nothing! We need nothing from those great clods! We are Tollins! We are . . . *nyaargh!* Yes, you seem to be leaning on it again. Would you mind moving off a bit? That stool *is* just for my leg, you know. I had it brought in specially. Well, there are other stools if you feel faint. If they're all taken, you must make do without mine. Yes, I'm quite sure.'

Bleary-eyed with pain, the High Tollin waved a hand in Sparkler's direction.

'To the cells with him. Execution in three days.'

CHAPTER THREE

NO HOPE AND NOTHING TO READ, EITHER

The cell was dark and damp and very far underground. The bars were wooden. Sparkler thought he could probably gnaw his way through them eventually, but he kept thinking that his parents would turn up at any moment and explain the quite silly mistake that had been made. They would all laugh and the High Tollin would pat him on the back and he would be allowed to go home.

He *had* spoken to humans of course. He knew there was the First Law, but it had been written when humans weren't using Tollins as industrial supplies. Surely an exception could be made for extreme circumstances? He sat in the black hole and waited for rescue or death, whichever came first.

As the hours, perhaps even days passed, he lost his sense that it would all be sorted out and grew slowly angrier. Imagine a marrow for a moment, in a garden. You don't see it happen, but it gets slowly bigger every hour. His temper was a bit like that, though probably impervious to snails.

When he heard footsteps, he was pacing the cell in fury at the stupidity of all High Tollins.

'Come to kill me have you?' he snapped. 'I won't go quietly, you know. I'll . . .'

'Shhh,' a voice came back, along with an odd scent of flowers. Sparkler took a step back.

'Who's there?' he asked. Had they come to torture him, perhaps immediately after bathing in lilac-scented water? No. Not those guards. Nettles, possibly. Lilacs, definitely not.

'Be quiet! The guards will hear you,' someone said. It was a female voice! It sounded a bit breathy, which Sparkler quite liked, though he thought that could be due to all those stairs leading down to the cells.

'I've come to get you out,' she said.

Sparkler was so angry by then that

he reacted the wrong way.

'Oh really? Perhaps I don't *want* to get out! Perhaps I would rather die for the cause of scientific knowledge—of all knowledge! Perhaps I would rather that Tollins everywhere remember that I gave my life for . . .'

'I have the keys, you know,' she interrupted. 'If you'd keep quiet for just a moment, I could find the right one for the lock. It isn't easy in the dark and you making speeches isn't helping.'

'Right. Sorry. I've been down here for a very long time.'

'Half the night, almost,' she agreed. The wooden keys clattered and the bars swung open.

'Where did you get the keys?' he asked. He still couldn't see her, but she was somewhere very close. He could still hear her breathing.

'From a key box,' she said, suddenly reluctant.

'But only the guards and the High Tollin have keys to the cells,' Sparkler whispered. He was pretty sure she couldn't be one of the guards, not with the smell of flowers. That left only one possibility.

'The High Tollin's key box? Are you the lady who wraps his foot?'

He heard a sigh in the darkness.

'I honestly thought this would be a bit more romantic,' she said. 'A midnight prison-break under the moonlight, a stolen kiss in the shadows . . .'

'Now hold *on*,' he said. 'I haven't even seen you. I mean, I'm grateful and everything, but for all I know you do this just for the kisses. Ow!'

The keys had come flying at him out of the darkness and he heard her steps vanishing into the tunnels. He could still smell the lilac though, which was nice.

He had to run. He had to do some serious thinking as well. He needed to reach the last place they would ever think to search.

CHAPTER FOUR

THE LAST PLACE THEY WOULD EVER THINK TO SEARCH

'Get out!' Grunion wailed, heaving at the little door. 'This is the *first* place they'll think to search.'

'No, it's the last place,' Sparkler declared, pushing on the door. 'They would never believe I'd return to the very spot where I was arrested.'

'They would! You did!' Grunion said, but he could not hold the door. Sparkler flung it back and raced away down the tunnel to the workshop.

'If I'm wrong and this is the first place they look, then I don't have much time.'

'They'll arrest me too,' Grunion said miserably, as he followed behind. 'I'll be all alone in a cell, except for you, and then it'll be out for execution and "whack whack", off with my head.'

Sparkler paused as Grunion caught up.

'Axes don't "whack", you know. You're thinking of some sort of stick. I think it will be more of a "chop chop", though I honestly don't know what it sounds like to the person being executed. I mean it could sound like quite a jolly swishing sound, then a sudden . . .' He stopped and looked along Grunion's shelves.

'A sudden what?' Grunion said.

'Hmm? Oh what does it matter, Grunion? It's almost dawn, I have a plan and I'm going to need your help!'

He held up the book of herbs. He had lost count of the time it had taken to copy each picture and every tiny word. He hardly needed them, they were so clear in his head, but he flicked through the pages and pointed in triumph.

'There, Grunion!' His voice fell almost to a whisper. 'The Purple Death!'

'It says "Autumn Crocus",' said Grunion, reading over his shoulder.

'Yes, Grunion, it *does* say "Autumn Crocus". Autumn Crocus is, in fact, what I need. However, there is no dramatic power in pointing to a page that could save my life and shouting "Autumn Crocus!" is there? Anyway, if you look in the footnotes, which were *incredibly* fiddly by the way, it is also known as . . . the Purple Death!' He paused again for effect, but Grunion didn't seem to appreciate it.

'You're going to *poison* someone?' said Grunion in horror.

'What? No! If you had actually bothered to read the book while I was in prison, you would have learned that all medicine is a balancing act between killing and curing.'

'And which one are you . . . ?'

'No time, Grunion. Follow me out onto the common. We must find this plant or perish.'

Grunion wasn't certain about being included in that 'we'. Only moments before, he had been cheerfully waiting for the kettle to boil and trying to get a bit of bread to stay on his toasting fork. It was more than tempting to close the door quietly behind Sparkler and go back to his breakfast. He stood there for a moment, looking down at his single slipper. It would surely be ruined in the snow. He sighed and set off after his friend.

Sparkler was alert for danger as he ran under the snow. Humans can run *over* snow, of course, leaving footprints. On cold days when their wings freeze up, Tollins have to dig straight through, under the surface. Sparkler was half frozen by the time he reached the little copse of trees that sheltered an even smaller patch of ground. He poked his head out of a snowdrift and looked around, his heart pounding. The sun was up and there were no foxes or owls to be seen. He took a deep breath as he heard Grunion slapping his way along the snow tunnel behind him.

The world was quiet as he made his way between two trees, searching the ground for the slightest hint of colour.

'Come on, come on,' he muttered. He'd seen them there, he was sure of it. Unless the snow had withered them . . . there!

'Here, Grunion!' he shouted, yanking at a fistful of purple petals. There was snow on some of the flowers and the cold was painful, but he didn't mind as he gave them to Grunion to hold.

They set off at a run back down the tunnel in the snow.

'But why did *I* have to come with you?' Grunion said irritably around his armful of petals. 'I could have put the kettle on the fire and be enjoying a nice fairy cake.'

Sparkler skidded to a stop. 'You wouldn't!' he said.

Grunion looked at him in confusion for a moment. 'Oh, I see,' he said. 'No, it's just a cake that fairies *made*, that's all. Nuts and fruit and things.'

'I should *hope* so,' Sparkler said.

Back in the warm workshop, Sparkler set to work, drying the petals on the fireplace and chopping them into small pieces. Outside, the sun had barely cleared the horizon when they heard a dull thumping on the outer door.

'I *told* you they'd come here first!' Grunion wailed. Sparkler stood up to his full height and put on a proud expression.

‘Let them in, friend Grunion. I am ready now,’ he said with great dignity.

‘Would you mind coming to the door instead? It’s just that if you wait there, they’ll track mud in.’

Sparkler deflated slightly.

‘Right. I will be ready at the door.’

CHAPTER FIVE

TEA AND EXECUTION

Hundreds of candles were lit in the hall of Tollins, deep under Chorleywood station. Above their heads, humans clumped their way to work and wished each other good morning, completely unaware of the desperate drama unfolding beneath their feet.

There had never been a prison break before. It was the talk of the hall, with lots of Tollins asking how it had been done. One of them knew, but she was saying nothing as she stood and eased her father's foot onto its special stool. The High Tollin winced and gasped as the swollen object thumped into place, but his eyes were bright with excitement.

'Bring him to me,' he shouted. The hall grew still. For a moment, the High Tollin thought the guards were struggling with the prisoner. In fact, they were trying to drag Sparkler in, but he was walking faster than they were and making it very difficult. As the High Tollin watched, one of them fell flat and rose with a furious expression.

Sparkler was bruised but unbowed. He had endured the sarcasm of the guards. He had even endured a brief and thorough experience of Community Guarding. (If he ever found himself alone with one of the guards and a sharp stick, that guard was going to be very sorry indeed.)

He saw the High Tollin was once again surrounded by his advisors. One of them had not been there before and Sparkler had a glimpse of blue eyes before she turned away. He thought he saw pity there and he would not be pitied, not that day.

The High Tollin brandished the wooden keys at him and Sparkler lifted his chin defiantly.

'How did you escape my cell, prisoner? What have you to say for yourself?'

'I say what I should have said the first time. I *have* learned from the humans, yes. I have learned many things that are useful for Tollins.'

The High Tollin frowned so hard his beard and eyebrows actually came together.

'You *dare*? You dare to plead your case when you are guilty not only of speaking to humans, but also of escaping my prison cells? Say how you did it and I will have the executioner go easy on you.'

Sparkler ignored the old Tollin's rage as well as his surprisingly vicious gestures with the ring of keys.

'I have copied out a book of herbs, a human book . . .'

'Executioner! Your biggest axe!' The High Tollin roared.

'In it, I have found that willow-bark can be used for headaches and to reduce fever. I have also found that the Autumn Crocus can ease gout when taken in small doses as a tea. It is said that . . .'

'Gout?' the High Tollin interrupted. The girl at his side beamed at Sparkler and he wasn't sure why. The High Tollin's gaze drifted over his enormous, swollen foot.

'He is lying to preserve 'is life, sah!' the guard said, worried by the sudden change of mood in the hall. He'd been looking forward to the biggest axe, as well.

Sparkler pulled out a pouch of the crocus petals and waved it at the High Tollin.

'I'm afraid it is human medicine, sir. I have learned its use by breaking our most sacred law. I quite understand if you wish the execution to go ahead.'

'Um . . .' the High Tollin said. He watched with beady eyes as Sparkler went over to the executioner, who was staggering with an axe far too large for him.

'Shall I stand, sir?' Sparkler said brightly, 'Or kneel?' He turned to the executioner Tollin, who wore a mask with little eye-holes. Unfortunately, the executioner had been summoned from his bed and he had the mask on back to front, so no one looked back.

'This herb cures gout, you say?' the High Tollin said, his voice a great deal quieter and more thoughtful.

'Not as fast as amputation,' Sparkler said. The High Tollin winced. His eyes were weary from pain and he looked longingly at the little pouch. Sparkler moved it back and forth and the old eyes followed.

'After studying the details of your case, I have decided that an exception can be made,' the High Tollin said solemnly. 'I grant you a pardon for all crimes.'

'Yessss!' his daughter said, grinning at Sparkler as her father went on.

'Perhaps I have indeed been rash. Perhaps Tollins and humans can learn to live together, to share their knowledge. We could all benefit from education. I am always saying that, aren't I, Wing?' His daughter nodded, blushing. 'An "Academy" is needed, a place where *all* knowledge is taught. I can see before me one bright young man who could be the very first professor. Over time, we . . .'

'No,' Sparkler said, firmly. The High Tollin paused, a dangerous light coming back into his eyes.

'What's that you say?'

'No, sir. Oh I like the idea of an Academy, of course. If there is to be a first professor, I recommend the healer, Grunion.' He took a deep breath. 'We spend our summers lying around drinking nectar and our winters growing thin. We can do better, but it won't be enough to depend on the humans to teach us. The Law should stand. We will find our way on our own.'

'But you said they know so much!' The High Tollin wailed.

Sparkler shrugged. 'We might catch them up, or learn different things, I don't know. I do know that we won't try to learn for ourselves if it's all just given to us. We must work for what we need. Let the Law stand and the humans go their own way. We are *not* humans. We are Tollins.'

The crowd applauded. Down by their feet, a fairy drew itself up to its full height. It talked of freedom and friendship, of forging bonds across the species. Unfortunately its voice was thin and squeaky and nobody noticed. As it reached a truly moving part about the rights of every fairy, someone stepped on it and its little voice was heard no more.

As the High Tollin's advisors rushed away to make Autumn Crocus tea, Sparkler smelled lilac and turned suddenly. The High Tollin's daughter Wing stood there, smiling shyly.

'It *was* you, wasn't it, with the keys?' he said.

'It was me.'

'Well if I'd known you were pretty, that would have been different! For all I knew you had a beard or something!'

She looked coldly at him for a long moment.

'You need to work on your compliments,' she said.

'I know!' Sparkler replied. 'There's still so much to learn!'

BOOK THREE

WINDBAGS
AND
DARK
TOLLINS

CHAPTER ONE

PURE RESEARCH AND THE PROBLEM WITH PUMPS

It was the middle of a golden summer and Chorleywood Common was filled with birds and insects and things, happily eating each other. Grasshoppers buzzed in the long grass; swallows swallowed, swifted or sometimes just sparrowed. An elderly heron stood on the edge of Darvell's Pond, watching the water as if it contained the secret of life itself.

Sparkler was on a field trip for the new Academy. An entire class of thirty young Tillets had come out on the common to hear him speak. Grunion had insisted they would all enjoy the experience and Sparkler could hardly refuse his old friend, no matter what else was worrying him. He pulled his thoughts together and tried to remember the question he had just been asked.

'As scientists, we never know the answers we are going to get. So we *test* the theories until we know. This is called the scientific method.'

Thirty small heads bobbed. Some made notes in tiny handwriting, while most of them just stared at him.

'Professor Grunion will be asking questions about this later, you know,' Sparkler said sternly. More heads dipped to write notes. Sparkler sighed as he saw one Tillet with her hand raised, yet again.

'Yes . . . Beryl, is it? You have a question?'

'Yeth. Why can't you just anthwer the quethtion you want to know? I mean if you want to find out why the thky ith blue, can't you work on that?'

Sparkler made a sound a little like 'hrumph' while he worked out what she had said. He had no idea why the sky was blue and as two other hands shot up, he spoke quickly to divert their attention.

'There is nothing wrong with that approach, young Beryl. Some problems must be solved as they come up. For example, I have a team working on a way to clear floodwater from the Hall of Tollins.' He sighed at the thought, wishing he were back there. 'But other scientists will do *pure* research, without looking for answers to anything.'

'Tho . . . they can never be wrong?' Beryl asked innocently. Sparkler shot her a sharp glance. He suspected she was brighter than she pretended.

'Well . . . yes, Beryl. You can't be *wrong* exactly. All you can do is disprove a theory.'

'Thounds like a good job, thir, if you can get it,' she said.

'Yes, I suppose it does,' Sparkler said, refusing to rise to the bait. 'For example, I have a theory that air actually weighs a great deal.'

'Oh, no, I don't think tho, thir.' Beryl raised her palm, flat. 'You thee, I can lift quite a lot of it and I'm not very thtrong.'

Sparkler could not mention that he had read the information in a human book. His memory of that stolen glance was vague. He too thought it was unlikely, in all honesty.

'Yes, Beryl, but if I am right, the heaviness of the air above us is something we just get used to.'

'Like a coat, thir?'

A Tillet lad looked up with interest. 'Made of wood, or something,' he said helpfully. 'A really heavy coat.'

'No, no not like a coat. Like a . . . like a blanket,' Sparkler said, beginning to sweat a bit.

'Made of wood,' the lad added.

'No.'

'You could tetht it by flying high up, I suppothe,' Beryl said doubtfully. 'To thee if the air ith lighter up there.'

Sparkler nodded. 'Very good, Beryl, but how high is high enough?' he said. 'Tollins are not high-flying creatures, as you know.'

Irritatingly, that was true. Tollins needed very little wing-power to go from flower to flower in the summer. Even bumble-bees make them look short-range. You may think flying things know a great deal about flight, but in fact the opposite is true. Bees *never* think about how they fly. If they did, they might crash into a rose bush.

'Pay attention, Tillets,' Sparkler said. 'Professor Grunion asked me to set homework, so here it is. How do we test if the air is less heavy up there?' Hands shot up, but the afternoon was waning and Sparkler was already thinking about the new arrivals in the tunnels under the station.

'Answers by tomorrow, please,' he said. 'Dis . . . wait for it, Beryl . . . dis . . . missed!'

The class lifted into the air and began making their way home. To Sparkler's satisfaction, many of them were looking up as they went.

* * *

The Hall of Tollins under Chorleywood station was still flooded by the time Sparkler returned. It had been flooded for the best part of a month, when the clumsy humans had dug some sort of a drain above their heads.

'How's the pump coming?' Sparkler asked his team, knowing the answer from their faces.

Wing was there, the daughter of the High Tollin himself. Sparkler wasn't sure how he felt about Wing. She was certainly pretty, but she seemed to regard him as some sort of puzzle she had to work out. He could feel her doing it as she looked at him. It was a little bit unnerving. She had an enormous brown mole as well. He didn't like it much, especially when it ate his sandwiches.

'It's still not watertight,' she said. 'You were right, pulling one wooden tube inside another seems to suck the water out of the tunnels. The problem is that we can't do it fast enough. Most of it leaks out and even if we empty the water into buckets, it will take years to drain the Hall.'

'More pumps?' Sparkler said, almost to himself. 'More Tollins on each pump? Rows of buckets?'

'Still too slow,' Wing said. 'It might be time to abandon the old Hall and make a new one.'

Sparkler sighed. He had vowed not to depend on human knowledge. Since he had cured the High Tollin's gout the previous winter, he had not been back to the book shelves in local houses. He had already copied a few to go with his herb book, but he had sworn that was it. Obviously he wished now he had not copied a French dictionary or the one about someone called Peter Pan. He'd only copied that because he thought it was about Tollins. The only really useful one was a book on ancient machines. If a giant catapult would have helped with the flood, Sparkler could have built it.

He was so engrossed in thought that he did not see the High Tollin's guards come up behind him. Now that he was a favourite of the High Tollin, they tried to be as nice as possible, hoping that he would perhaps forget the rough treatment when he was just an escaped prisoner.

'Message for you, sah,' said the larger one. 'The High Tollin most respectfully requests your presence.'

'What, now?' Sparkler said. 'I'm in the middle of trying to work out . . .'

'You'd better go,' Wing said. 'You know what Dad can be like and he's already busy with those Dark Tollins.'

Sparkler frowned at the unpleasant reminder.

'Yes, I suppose so. Lead on then.'

The guard nodded, smiling greasily.

'Right you are, your honour.'

Chapter Two

WHY ROAST BEETLE IS ALWAYS THE RIGHT CHOICE

As Sparkler entered the temporary Great Hall, which wasn't a hall and certainly wasn't great, he noticed the High Tollin smiling across at him, which was always a worrying sign. Around the bearded old prune were the newcomers: Dark or Country Tollins. It wasn't that Sparkler disliked them, not exactly. The whole Tollin community of Chorleywood was in a buzz about them. Visitors were rare enough and the Dark Tollins had come up from Dorset, further to the south than almost any of them had ever been, even by firework.

The Dark Tollins hadn't been impressed by the pumps, which was fair enough as they didn't work. They also hadn't been impressed by curing gout or the classes for young Tillets. Sparkler had the strong impression that they thought he was a troublemaker, intent on upsetting the proper Tollin ways. Still, it was only a visit. They couldn't stay forever.

'Come in, young Sparkler,' the High Tollin said cheerfully. 'I'm sorry we can't offer you a chair, but this room is rather cramped compared to the old Hall.'

Sparkler nodded a greeting to the newcomers. They stood very close to the High Tollin, almost as if they owned him. Sparkler struggled to put a smile on his face. The sooner this was over, the sooner he could go back to the problem of the pumps.

'You called for me, sir?' he said.

'To introduce you, lad. You haven't met our country cousins yet? Good, good. This young man, gentlemen, is our finest asset! A boy of great promise and wondrous brain!'

The leader of the Dark Tollins stepped forward and made a short bow. He was dressed in simple clothes, well worn. He looked curiously at Sparkler, but spoke to the High Tollin.

'We've heard about this one, of

course. The Tollin who speaks to humans and steals from them. The one who cares nothing for the old ways.'

The High Tollin froze in shock.

'That's a bit much, Wangle, don't you think? A bit rude?'

Sparkler felt a flush of anger spoiling his calm.

'You think it's enough to laze around all summer, then starve all winter, do you?' he demanded.

'Now, now, Sparkler, there is no need to get upset,' said the High Tollin. 'I'm sure our guest did not mean to offend. I thought you could perhaps show him your progress with the pumps. The old Hall will be dry and snug any day now, I'm certain.'

'Tollins built the first Great Hall,' Wangle said coldly. 'Tollins can build another, with their own hands. *True* Tollins don't need these pomps.'

'That's "pumps",' said Sparkler wearily. 'And yes, we could just dig another hole, but we have more brains than moles or badgers. You let yours turn to soup, if you like. *This* Tollin will embrace the future.'

'Be careful what you embrace, Tollin,' Wangle said. 'Some things have thorns.'

*   *   *

The following evening, Sparkler was pacing the workshop of his friend Grunion. The smell of roasted beetle filled the air.

'The nerve of him, Grunion! He'd have us grubbing about in the mud forever, I suppose.' As he paced, Sparkler looked through the homework his temporary class had handed in. Even the fact that the paper had come from his own experiments with grasses was a reminder of the scornful Dark Tollins.

'A hawk!' he said, throwing one piece of the grasspaper down. 'Oh yes, very sensible. We attach ourselves to a hawk and somehow persuade it to fly very high.'

He looked at the next one, Beryl's entry.

'Why are they called Dark Tollins, anyway?' Grunion asked, chewing on a bit of leg. 'Needs something, this beetle, perhaps a bit of wild onion.'

'Hmm? Oh, they're called Dark Tollins because they prefer tunnels to daylight. I don't think they even use flowers. Just a life in the dark, eating worms and things. Our cousins! Honestly, we have more in common with fairies. At least *they* don't live like moles.' He accepted a leg and crunched it as he read. That was the good thing about roasted beetle. Always enough leg for everyone.

'This one from Beryl is interesting,' said Sparkler, reading. 'Fire sparks move upwards, but fall when they are cold, so hot things must rise . . . A fire could be carried in a clay pot to heat the air . . .' He thought for a time. 'It's an interesting idea. We'd need some way to catch the hot air—a bag of some kind. Hmm . . . if we carry the heat with us, in theory, we should be able to just keep going up forever.'

'Until you hit the sky, obviously,' said Grunion, munching.

'I don't think you can "hit" anything, Grunion. It's just sky—air, you know.'

‘How do you know though? Could be glass, or something.’

Sparkler’s eyes gleamed.

‘It’s a theory,’ he murmured. ‘The question is, can we test it?’

Chapter Three

HIGH HOPES

They didn't call it a balloon. That is a human word and just means a big ball. The class of Tillets called it a windbag and kept giggling about the name for reasons Sparkler could not understand.

It was simple enough to make, once he had persuaded the old Tollin ladies to sew great ovals of grasspaper together. The danger of course was that it could be seen. Humans are not good at spotting Tollins, but they would have no problem seeing a small hot-air balloon rise slowly above the common. As a result, most of the stitching had been done in the chambers under the station, then brought out in pieces. Sparkler gritted his teeth as the Dark Tollins came round to examine the work. Their leader sneered when he heard it was for flying.

'You'll be making legs for walking

next,' Wangle murmured, almost to himself, but just loud enough for Sparkler to hear. He didn't reply. His father had always said he should rise above insults and this time, with his windbag, he was going to take the advice literally.

They chose dawn for the first flight, when very few humans would be about. Sparkler found a spot deep in the woods and instructed the class in tying the string to a wooden spindle. The design for a catapult had come in useful after all, as he had a way to unwind the string slowly.

'You turn the handle click by click, understand?' he said to the Tillet boy who seemed to think the air was a wooden blanket. The boy nodded, proud to be included.

Sparkler was the only one going up in the small basket underneath the wind bag. He didn't see how it could be dangerous, but he'd refused Beryl's request to come along.

The candles in the tray sent hot air into the bag and slowly, wonderfully, it grew plump. The basket trembled on the ground and, with Beryl watching, Sparkler tried to look as if he wasn't enjoying himself.

'Hold on!' came a voice he knew. It was Wing, flying low over the grasses.

Sparkler looked nervously at the class, who nudged each other.

'Um . . . yes?' he said. Wing rolled her eyes.

'I'm coming too,' she said.

'There's no room,' Sparkler replied, 'Settle down, class.'

'Yes there is, look,' Wing said, climbing in. 'Pop another candle in the tray if it needs it. I have sandwiches as well. And a kettle, to make tea.'

'Sandwiches?' Sparkler said. 'Wing, this is science, not an outing!'

'No, it's more of an upping than an outing, but even scientist Tollins need sandwiches.'

'Not the kettle then, we'll never get off the ground.'

'Scientists need tea as well,' she said firmly.

Beryl was grinning for some reason and Sparkler gave up. He put another two extra candles in the tray and lit them from the others. The windbag began to quiver again.

'One click at a time,' Sparkler called to the Tillet on the winch. 'Gently does it.'

'This is fun,' Wing murmured, making herself comfortable.

'It's science, Wing!' Sparkler hissed.

'Fun too, though,' she said.

The wooden spindle turned and the long woven thread unwound, click by careful click. The windbag lifted into the air, taking two Tollins, some sandwiches and a kettle. Some of the Tillets said, 'Oooh!' at the sight, while others said, 'Aaaah!'

Slowly, the windbag rose above the trees and still further, so that the class of Tillets was just a distant smudge on the ground.

'I should have worked out a signal,' Sparkler said suddenly. 'How will they know when to bring us down again?'

'We could always fly down and tell them,' Wing said.

'Not if we go as high as I'd like,' he replied. 'There's an awful lot of thread down there, you know. I did tell you this wasn't just a day out.'

'Still, it's very peaceful,' she said. 'And I don't often get you to myself.'

Sparkler cleared his throat, feeling a bit warm despite the breeze. The trees grew smaller below and for a time, he was lost in appreciating the view. He'd never been so high. He doubted any Tollin ever had.

'Those Dark Tollins would eat their words if they could see this!' he said.

The basket lurched and Wing cried out, grabbing the edge.

'What was that?' she said.

They seemed to be rising much faster all of a sudden.

'Oh no,' Sparkler said. The windbag was shooting upwards.

'The string must have broken,' he said. The common was just a green patch below them and he could have sworn it was getting colder. The clouds were still above them. Surely they couldn't rise above the clouds? He winced at the thought of bumping the windbag on the glass ceiling Grunion had predicted.

'What do we do?' Wing said. Her

voice was surprisingly calm, so Sparkler calmed down as well. She handed him a sandwich and he chewed it thoughtfully.

'Too high to fly down ourselves, do you think?' he said.

'I don't know. We could do it in *theory*, but who wants to test that?'

The air became white mist as they reached the clouds. For a time, the two Tollins were blind as they rose higher and higher.

'You're shivering,' Wing said. 'I should have brought a blanket.'

Sparkler was thinking, hard.

'I can snuff the candles and the air in the bag should cool. We'd come down again.'

'How fast?' Wing asked seriously.

'I have no idea,' he said.

'Then I'll put the kettle on the candles while you're making your mind up,' she said. 'Are we going to die?'

'I don't know!' Sparkler said miserably.

'Definitely cup of tea time, then.'

'How could the string have broken?' he said.

* * *

Far below, the Tillets were flying in all directions, panicked. The Dark Tollins stood by the winch, looking up at the tiny speck that was the windbag being swallowed in clouds. Wangle sheathed a dagger and dropped the severed thread.

'Right. That's him out of the way,' he said sourly. 'Too many ideas for his own good. Are the others ready?'

'They are,' said another. 'We have the High Tollin and that means we have them all in the palms of our hands.'

'Get them building a new Great Hall then. Fit for a Dark High Tollin.'

'Or a High Dark Tollin, if you like,' his companion said.

'Just get them *digging*, will you?' Wangle replied.

Chapter Four

HIGH TEA

Breaking through the clouds would have been a wonderful experience, if Sparkler hadn't been close to panic. By the time the tea was boiling and he had snuffed all but one of the candles, the clouds themselves were far below.

'This tea is tepid,' he said.

'Well the kettle boiled,' Wing said. 'It should be piping hot.'

'Really?' Sparkler replied. She shrugged and put the kettle back on the last candle, wedging it on the wooden struts. In just moments, the water was boiling and she took the lid off to show him. Sparkler threw away his tea and poured more water, sipping it warily.

'What are you *doing*?' Wing cried.

'*Still* not hot!' Sparkler said in wonder. 'It must be the height. No, the weight of the air! There's less air above us, Wing! Somehow, having less weight changes something important and the water bubbles at a lower temperature. [*Surprisingly, this is true.*] If only I could freeze it, to see what happens then. This is wonderful! Beryl will be thrilled. Wing, we need to get down, right now!'

She watched him stare at the steaming kettle for a while, lost in thought. He really was a very odd Tollin indeed, but she hadn't met another like him.

Wing reached out and snuffed the last candle.

'Right then. Let's hope it's slow enough to jump out before we hit the ground,' she said.

'Oh, this is brilliant,' Sparkler said, dreamily. His mind was hopping from idea to idea like one of the droplets hissing on the kettle. 'Steam, Wing. For the pumps. I can use steam!'

'Yes, that's lovely,' she said. The windbag seemed to be rising more slowly, or even not rising at all. The world below was enormous, bigger than she'd ever realised. She swallowed nervously as they began to descend.

*   *   *

Deep under Chorleywood station, the High Tollin was purple with rage.

'You will *regret* this! You came here to steal our tunnels, our homes! You use us like slaves. *Sla-aves*! You're worse than the bearded men. Execution is too good for you!'

'Do be quiet, old fellow,' Wangle said. 'You think we country cousins are simple folk? What did that boy say? 'Lazing in the sun and starving in winter?' Yes, and we are *tired* of it. For an entire year, we hear stories of the clever Tollins under the station, who can cure disease and make paper. Why should we grow thin and ill while you are fat and healthy?'

'But we would have helped you if you'd asked!' said the High Tollin, indignantly. He tried to rattle his chains in fury, but they were made of wood and the sound was actually quite pleasant.

'Would you? Perhaps you would.

This way is more certain. Your tunnels are mine, your people are mine. Everything you have learned will be mine as well. Now do quieten down, or I'll find a gag for you.'

The High Tollin glared at him. He *had* thought of the Dark Tollins as simple folk, yes. The ones who stood ready to answer Wangle's orders did not look simple at all. They looked large and bony and they glared at him. In turn, he glared at his two guards, who were chained and gagged in the corner. They glared at each other.

Wangle smiled at the High Tollin's frustration as he turned to his Dark advisors.

'How is the new Hall coming along?' he said.

'Very nicely, my lord. They're hard workers, I'll give them that. It should be finished in a week.'

'Excellent. When it is complete, I will be appointed High Dark Tollin for Chorleywood.'

'Or . . . the "Dark High Tollin" if you like.'

'Is this important *now*, do you

think?'

'No, my lord.'

Chapter Five

LOW PLOTS AND HOT WATER

The tunnels under the station were damp and echoey as Sparkler, Wing and Grunion crept along them, bowed almost double by their burdens.

'Keep an eye out for guards,' Sparkler whispered. He was still limping after twisting his ankle as the balloon came down, but he ignored the pain.

Grunion groaned under the weight of equipment. Sparkler had been like a Tollin possessed ever since the wind bag had come down. Grunion's small workshop had become the centre for the resistance, which seemed to be just the three of them.

Each night, Wing had crept back to the tunnels under the station and watched in horror as the Dark Tollins forced her people to keep working by torchlight.

As the days passed, Grunion had

suffered a constant fog of boiling water while Sparkler experimented with his new pump. At last it was finished and Grunion was sure he had all the heaviest bits on his back.

They came to the old Hall of Tollins, where the tunnels were still flooded and crumbling into the muck.

'This will do, Grunion. Put it all down now, but gently,' Sparkler whispered. They had practiced many times in the workshop and even in darkness, the machine slotted together quickly.

'This is the most dangerous part,' Sparkler said to Wing. 'If the Dark Tollins smell the fire and come looking, we're sunk.'

'Don't worry, they're over at the new Great Hall, preparing,' she muttered back. 'We should have been prepared for *them*, you know. How could they just walk in and take over the whole community? If Grunion didn't live out by the pond, we'd have been lost.'

'We trusted them, but that is a problem for another day,' said Sparkler firmly. He took a shuttered lantern and removed the candle from it, casting odd shadows on the walls of the tunnel. With that, he lit the boiler for his pump and nodded in appreciation as he closed the opening.

'That should do it. When the steam rises, it will hit the second chamber and condense once again. The inner tube should be sucked up into the outer one, drawing floodwater into the hosepipe.'

'The hosepipe!' Grunion said suddenly. 'I've left it behind!'

'Run and get it, then!' Wing snapped. The tension was unbearable. They could already feel the pump getting hot from within. Grunion set off, the tap-thump of his wooden foot echoing from the walls.

'This is bad,' Sparkler said. 'Without that pipe, we have no plan.'

* * *

In the new Hall of Tollins, Wangle walked slowly, dressed in a long robe that trailed on the floor behind him.

'Then I will make a speech,

welcoming a new age of Tollins and so on and so on,' he said. 'You will hand me the crown and Albert here will put it on my head. That will be official.'

The High Tollin shook his head. He hated to be called by his real name and his eyebrows quivered in indignation.

'I won't do it! You are traitors, all of you!'

'You *will* do it, Albert.' Wangle turned to his advisors. 'He has a daughter, does he not?'

'Oh yes, my lord. Girl with a mole.'

'I'm sorry?'

'A brown one, my lord. It's vicious, if you want to know the truth. It nearly had my fingers off when I tried to stroke it.'

Wangle blinked as he considered this.

'I see . . .' he said. 'High Tollin, if you do not do as I say . . . is it a pet, then? Are we talking about a pet?'

'Yes, my lord,' said the advisor.

'Right. Clear at last. High Tollin, if you do not do as I say, I will have your daughter fed to an owl. Is that clear enough for you?'

For a moment, Wangle heard a peculiar sound, like a man running past the open door with some sort of wooden clog on. He peered out into the darkness.

'And get some more candles lit. This is meant to be a joyous occasion,' he said.

'I have it!' Grunion hissed from the darkness. 'I have the hosepipe!'

He handed it over. Sparkler breathed in relief as he screwed it to the pump.

'It's almost ready,' he said. 'I just wish I could know how fast the water is going to come out. Wood and pottery is not good enough for this. If I had iron . . .'

'There's something else,' Grunion said. 'It's your father, Wing. He's in the new Hall, with the Dark Tollins. I'm sorry.'

Wing gasped.

'I can still throw cold water on the boiler and shut it down,' Sparkler said. 'We'll think of something else, Wing.'

'No,' she said softly. 'No we won't. I know what my father would say if I asked him.'

'Are you sure?' Sparkler said. 'It could mean his life . . .'

'Yes, I am.'

'Good, because I think the pump is just about to . . .'

With a *whoosh*, water started spurting out of the hosepipe. In just moments, it went from being a long tube made from the intestines of an unlucky field-mouse, to a writhing snake. All three of them grabbed it and held on as it bucked, sending a torrent of water blasting down the tunnel with a noise like a little boy sucking a gobstopper.

In the distance, they could hear cries of alarm, but the water kept coming, emptying out the old Hall of Tollins and pouring the water down the tunnel into the new one.

Without warning the water died to a trickle.

'What's gone wrong?' Wing said, desperately. She could hear Dark Tollins running towards them, determined to stop this strange machine.

'Don't worry, it's just the second stage,' Sparkler said. 'The machine sort of sucks in a breath, you see, then . . .'

He was interrupted by the Dark Tollins, all yelling. They yelled a bit more when the water came on again, washing them back down into the new Great Hall.

The Hall filled with extraordinary speed as the pump groaned and creaked and spat hot droplets of water. Half the chambers under the station were flooded and one by one, the water was drawn away from them, pouring into the Dark High Hall, or the High Dark Hall, if you like.

Quickly, the waters drained from the flooded new Hall. Its earth walls could not hold water like the polished clay of the old one and as the flood dribbled away, there was no sign of the Dark Tollins.

Sparkler and Wing entered the muddy chamber. Behind them, the other Tollins were coming out of hiding, understanding that at last the terror was over.

'I suppose they were washed away,

down other tunnels,' Sparkler said. He saw Wing looking around desperately, but there was no sign of her father. The mud was almost too deep to wade through and the chamber would take weeks to dry out. Sparkler thought he heard her sob and he put his arm around her.

'We'll find him, Wing. Of course we will. They won't be back, you know. They couldn't take us by surprise another time anyway. Not now we're ready.'

Behind him, a shape stirred in the mud, rising up like a monster from the beginning of time. Wooden chains clicked and slithered as it shuffled forward, its eyes red and blinking.

'Wing?' said the monster.

'Dad!' she cried, rushing to embrace him.

'Have you seen my guards?' he asked. 'They were chained up and gagged when the flood came. I do hope . . .'

'Gag fell orf, sah,' came a voice from a pile of sludge. 'Which was a shame, as I was almost finished biting through it.'

'And your companion?' the High Tollin asked, still dazed.

'Under me, sah, but it's all right. I can still feel him wrigglin'. I do believe the chains saved us, sah. Kept us afloat, sah.'

'Splendid. Will you be able to report to the executioner this afternoon?'

'Dad!' Wing said, shocked. Her father sighed and spat a bit of mud out.

'Oh all right. It's been a difficult day.'

*   *   *

A week later, Sparkler looked round for Wing as he walked through the old Great Hall of Tollins. It was dry as a bone and the floor had been polished specially. On all the galleries above, the crowd went 'Berserk!', with perfect timing, showing that you *can* take instructions too literally. They tried going 'Wild!' as well, but after that, they just cheered in their own time.

The High Tollin was in an expansive mood as he patted the air for quiet. His daughter's mole lunged at his fingers and had to be pulled back on its leash.

'We are gathered here to honour a fine young Tollin. He saved us from slavery. *Sla-avery*! He cured my gout. He saved us from the Dark Tollins. He made a pump. He is truly an extraordinary Tollin. Accordingly, I have created the Order of the Owl in his honour. Step forward, that brave Tollin.'

Sparkler stepped forward, blushing, and bowed his head as Wing's father put a small ribbon around his neck. He did not look at the medal on the ribbon, as he knew it very well already. It was the first metal item from the new blast furnace. As he had said to Grunion, the future was bright. The future was metal.